ELITE FORCES SELECTION

SPECIAL FORCES: PROTECTING, BUILDING, TEACHING, AND FIGHTING

ELITE FORCES SELECTION

by Jack Montana

Mason Crest Publishers

MASON CREST PUBLISHERS INC.
370 Reed Road
Broomall, Pennsylvania 19008
(866)MCP-BOOK (toll free)
www.masoncrest.com

First Printing
9 8 7 6 5 4 3 2 1

Library of Congress Cataloging-in-Publication Data

Montana, Jack.
  Elite forces selection / by Jack Montana.
    p. cm. — (Special forces : protecting, building, teaching and fighting)
  Includes bibliographical references and index.
  ISBN 978-1-4222-1839-6   ISBN (series) 978-1-4222-1836-5
  1. Special forces (Military science)—United States—Juvenile literature. 2. United States—Armed Forces—Commando troops—Juvenile literature. 3. Physical fitness—Juvenile literature. 4. Mental health—Juvenile literature. I. Title.
  UA34.S64M38 2011
  356'.16—dc22
                              2010016871

Produced by Harding House Publishing Service, Inc.
www.hardinghousepages.com
Interior design by MK Bassett-Harvey.
Cover design by Torque Advertising + Design.
Printed in USA by Bang Printing.

With thanks and appreciation to the U.S. Military for the use of information, text, and images.

Contents

Introduction

Elite forces are the tip of Freedom's spear. These small, special units are universally the first to engage, whether on reconnaissance missions into denied territory for larger conventional forces or in direct action, surgical operations, preemptive strikes, retaliatory action, and hostage rescues. They lead the way in today's war on terrorism, the war on drugs, the war on transnational unrest, and in humanitarian operations as well as nation building. When large-scale warfare erupts, they offer theater commanders a wide variety of unique, unconventional options.

Most such units are regionally oriented, acclimated to the culture and conversant in the languages of the areas where they operate. Since they deploy to those areas regularly, often for combined training exercises with indigenous forces, these elite units also serve as peacetime "global scouts," and "diplomacy multipliers," beacons of hope for the democratic aspirations of oppressed peoples all over the globe.

Elite forces are truly "quiet professionals": their actions speak louder than words. They are self-motivated, self-confidant, versatile, seasoned, mature individuals who rely on teamwork more than daring-do. Unfortunately, theirs is dangerous work. Since the 1980 attempt to rescue hostages from the U.S. embassy in Tehran, American special operations forces have suffered casualties in real-world operations at close to fifteen times the rate of U.S. conventional forces. By the very nature of the challenges that face special operations forces, training for these elite units has proven even more hazardous.

Thus it's with special pride that I join you in saluting the brave men who volunteer to serve in and support these magnificent units and who face such difficult challenges ahead.

—*Colonel John T. Carney, Jr., USAF–Ret.*
President, Special Operations Warrior Foundation

CHAPTER 1

Getting Fit

Five weeks after the terrorist attacks of September 11, 2001, a handful of Special Forces soldiers landed in Afghanistan and began special operations. On horseback, with the help of locals, they were able to help topple the Taliban in two months. Many had expected this phase of the war to last as long as a year.

The Special Forces achievement required not only technical ability but also language and cultural skills to work with **counterinsurgency**; cultural sensitivity was as important as the ability to shoot a machine gun. And physical fitness was essential.

The members of elite forces units must train their bodies for maximum endurance and strength. If Special Forces

UNDERSTAND THE FULL MEANING

counterinsurgency: A program focused on working against a rebellion or rebellious elements within a government.

soldiers do not have healthy bodies, they will most likely fail in their mission.

WHY IS PHYSICAL FITNESS SO IMPORTANT?

The healthier you are, the more likely you will be to fully enjoy life. Protecting your health also helps you avoid illness and injuries. Medical science shows that people who stay fit and eat healthy live longer. In the extreme situations elite soldiers face, being fit and healthy becomes even more important. It can make the difference between living and dying.

Much of the advice in this book applies to civilian life as well. Staying fit can help combat the negative effects of stress on the body, whether you're facing the challenges of military life or the ordinary challenges of daily life. If you suffer from a poor appetite, interrupted sleep, feelings of

DID YOU KNOW?

If you begin every exercise program with a gentle warm-up and stretching exercises, blood starts to flow to the muscles and you can avoid muscle tears and strained ligaments. Also, after a tough exercise session, cool down with a series of gentle exercises so your body can return to normal. These practices will help you be more supple.

Proper stretching before and after a work-out is important for the most effective exercise program. These soldiers are stretching their quads as part of their routine cool down after a 5K (3.1 m) run.

If your goal is to be in the Special Forces, here's a work-out schedule that may help you reach it:

- Swim two to three times a week, 1,000 to 2,000 meters each time. One day a week, try to swim wearing cammies and boots for 100 meters. NEVER swim alone.

- Run four to five times a week, 3 to 5 miles (5–8 km) as fast as you can. Once a week, do rucksack marches carrying a 50-pound (22.5-kg) load.

- Every other day do 75–100 pull-ups (7–10 sets of 10 reps); 200–300 push-ups, (10–15 sets of 20 reps); and 200–300 sit-ups (5–10 sets of 40–50 reps).

unease, or a general lack of confidence, getting in shape can help.

Fitness includes three categories: suppleness, stamina, and strength. Suppleness is the ability to stretch your body, stamina is the ability to resist tiredness, and strength is the

DID YOU KNOW?

If you start to experience chest-pains, pains shooting up the arms, problems with breathing, sweating, or headaches, see your doctor. Understand the difference between feeling mild pain from stress and the piercing, sharp pain of dealing with an injury. Also learn to categorize levels of pain. If you do deal with an injury, being able to explain the amount of pain as well as kind of pain will help the doctor help you get better.

total power you can exert with your body. Younger people place an emphasis on strength and stamina; older people often want to improve their suppleness. In reality, suppleness is important for all of us, and for the elite forces, it is especially important in self-defense, where high kicks are often needed. Running speed and fighting power also depend on a high degree of suppleness.

PACE YOURSELF

Too much exercise too soon can lead to an injury. Begin gradually building up the speed and number of times you repeat an exercise. If you haven't exercised for some time, start by taking fast walks. The little things make a difference: for instance, walking home from school rather than taking a bus. Take the stairs instead of the elevator. Walk to the store rather than take the car.

If you build a little more exercise into every day, you will soon experience the benefits. Do not be discouraged by the initial discomfort; it is always hard work at the beginning. You will soon get into a routine, and the aches will disappear as your fitness increases.

When trying to get fit, join a good gym (if your school does not have its own facilities that you can use for free). Visit different gyms before making your selection. Of course, you can train at home but lack of space may be a problem. In good weather you can use the backyard. Self-motivation is another problem: at home there are no gym instructors to spur you on.

WARM UP

Before doing any hard exercise, warm up to prevent your muscles from becoming damaged. Mild exercise like jogging is an ideal warm-up. Pay attention to all the muscles in your body. Walking, swimming, and cycling are ideal ways to warm-up, as long as you take it gently. The general idea is to raise the pulse and get blood circulating faster. The amount of time you need to spend warming up depends on the temperature of the place you are exercising. In warm temperature, you should warm up for a minimum of six minutes; on a cold day you need to exercise for at least twelve minutes.

Here is a good way to warm up using the running track in a regular gym:

- For the first three laps, run on your toes and lift your knees high.

- On the fourth lap, start to exercise the arms, punching the arms high in the air, first with the left arm and then the right arm.

- On lap five, face inward and run sideways, leading with the left leg. Halfway through the lap, face outward so that your right leg leads.

- On lap six, hop for 3 feet on one leg, then change to the other leg and repeat.

- On lap seven, run backward for half a lap and then forward again, punching your arms above your head. (Watch where you're going!)

U.S. Navy Pre-Basic Underwater Demolition/SEAL training students run laps as part of their physical training.

- After seven laps, stand with your legs a shoulder's width apart, with your hands on hips and elbows slightly forward. Breathe deeply and slowly, in through the nose and out the mouth. This warm-up period helps soldiers prevent injury and prepares the body for more demanding exercise. You should never skip the warm-up. Elite soldiers do it before every exercise routine.

Once the body is warmed up, it is time to stretch your muscles, tendons, and ligaments to improve overall mobility and help flexibility. When stretching, always start at the top and work down the body. You must learn stretches from a fitness instructor; if they're not done properly you can hurt yourself. Ask your coach, trainer, or physical therapy trainer for more information on how to stretch. The most important thing to remember is not to stretch too hard. Stop if you feel pain while stretching.

Exercise must be fun; otherwise you will not want to continue doing it regularly. Try to exercise with a group of friends. Exercising to music can make exercise more enjoyable as well. Exercise is hard work, but anything worth doing has a price. The more you exercise, the easier it becomes.

TRAINING

While training for elite forces selection, focus on speed, strength, and endurance.

CALISTHENICS

Calisthenics are a form of exercises that consist of simple, repetitive movements performed without weights. Calisthenics are intended to increase body strength and flexibility. These are rigid, military-type, "parade ground" exercises, designed to promote straight backs, raised chests, and a shoulders-back physique. Elite soldiers take pride in themselves and want to look and feel like a soldier.

ANAEROBIC EXERCISE

Anaerobics are exercises that build muscle through tension. They do not increase the heart rate as dramatically as aero-

U.S. Marines perform calisthenics before a training run.

bic exercise. Anaerobic activities tend to be fast, furious, and short, and you generally do not get out of breath. They include martial arts and sprinting for short distances (no more than 100 meters). Anaerobic exercises are good for building up muscle strength but not good for endurance—you need aerobic exercises for that.

AEROBIC EXERCISE

Most exercise is aerobic, which means it requires oxygen. Aerobic exercises make your heart beat faster and your lungs breathe deeper. They also include endurance workouts such as rowing, cycling, and swimming, plus the longer track events such as the 800- and 1500-meter run. Aerobic exercise helps build up heart and lung strength. A strong heart and lungs are needed to do well in the elite forces.

CIRCUIT TRAINING

Circuit training involves doing lots of different exercises that strengthen all parts of the body. In one part of the gym you might jog on the spot, then run to another spot where you do stomach exercises. Circuits often use weights and exercise machines.

WEIGHT TRAINING

This increases performance by increasing overall strength, an important quality for elite forces soldiers who often have to carry heavy weights into battle (sometimes their packs and rifles can add up to 80 pounds [36 kg] in weight). Most gyms and some schools have weight rooms, but make sure an instructor shows you how to use the equipment.

While weight training is important, using weights is not required to succeed in training.

BE YOUR BEST

The Special Forces insist on excellence. Learn to settle for nothing less for yourself. This means being in the best physical shape you can possibly be—but it also means being at your best mentally.

Advice from the Expert

Stew Smith is a graduate of the U.S. Naval Academy, a former Navy SEAL, and the author of several fitness and self-defense books, as well as a military fitness trainer. Here are his 10 top tips for getting yourself in shape for the Special Forces:

1. Be motivated.

It is no one's job but yours to motivate you to serve your country. You have to be motivated and understand that your fitness level could be the difference between life and death for you, your partner, or a victim you are attempting to save.

2. Build your upper body strength.

Make sure you can do push-ups, sit-ups, and even pull-ups of some form, as these exercises will help you climb fences or ropes, jump walls, and handle an opponent if needed. Practice with weights, walls, ropes, and fences. Do not assume that you can accomplish these skills without practice.

3. Don't settle for minimum standards.

It is your job to use or create a plan that will prepare you well within the minimum physical standards of the unit you choose to serve. Minimum standards never helped anyone excel in training. Minimum standards are like getting a "D" on academic work. It is passing but getting through to the next level or training is going require much more work. Statistics show the better you score on the entrance fitness test, the better you are at completing the course of instruction well.

4. Be able to run.

You do not have to have marathon experience, but a minimum of 15–20 miles a week is a great base to handle your training programs without over-use injuries like shin splints, stress fractures, joint tendonitis, and others.

5. Know the specialty tests.

Each unit has certain tests you will have to pass—and it is your job to do the research and find out what is expected of you during and after training. For instance, if you are planning on joining the Navy, practice swimming. If you want to join the Army, run; then put a backpack on and walk fast (ruck march). Practice running stairs, sprints, climbing walls, dragging something heavy.

6. Be a team player.

When you are going through training, you will be assessed on how well you work with others. Following orders as well as developing ideas and sharing them with your team are critical skills that you should be able to perform without thinking. If you are in high school, play team sports, join the band, do community action groups. Do something that will help you learn these skills now.

7. Learn the ranks.

This is a little less physically demanding, but if you do not know the ranking system as well as other historical information about your unit, its famous people, and its heroes, it is likely you will pay the price in push-ups and other extra physically demanding duties. There is a saying in many training programs, "If you are going to be stupid, you'd better be strong."

8. Eat right for energy (and don't drink).

Eating good carbohydrates and protein-rich foods like fruits, veggies, and lean meats is the best tool for energy to exercise. Too many people rely on energy drinks that are really just caffeine and sugar; they spike your central nervous system but don't provide proper sustainable fuel for workouts.

9. Show up for training within weight standards.

Being heavy or overweight will likely challenge you to work harder when running, doing obstacle courses, and staying up with the class physically. If you are one of those bigger muscle guys, someone who is lean but big, your strength and power will come in handy, but don't let it hamper your cardiovascular endurance. Big guys can run a 6–7-minute-mile too; you just have to work at it prior to your training.

10. Did I mention run?

Make sure you can run. You will run from one place to another, usually carrying your gear for that event. Running injuries are typically the number-one issue for people attending boot camps and special ops units.

(Adapted from www.military.com/fitness-center/military-fitness/stew-smith/archive.)

CHAPTER 2
Peaceful Warriors: Preparing the Mind

Philosopher Baruch Spinoza wrote, "Peace is not the absence of war; it is a virtue; a state of mind; a **disposition** for **benevolence**; confidence; and justice." We need to be in a peaceful state of mind when training to wage war.

Elite forces need to be in good physical shape, and they receive plenty of practical training as well. But one of the most important skills they need to learn is how to handle stress. To show your superiors that you are able to handle performing an actual mission you need a clear mind. This means that you

UNDERSTAND THE FULL MEANING

disposition: A person's basic outlook, mood, and emotional state.

benevolence: Kindness, compassion, the desire to do good.

Is This Right for Me?

Often military leaders say that if you have any question about whether or not you should join the Special Forces, you shouldn't. This oversimplifies the question. After all, you need to ask questions before you can make a decision.

Here are some of the questions that might help you decide on whether a career in the Special Forces is right for you:

Do you enjoy working in a team?
Do you hate to miss a workout?
Do you enjoy being in the wilderness?
Can you cope with crises without falling apart emotionally?

If you answered "yes" to these questions, you could be a good candidate for the Special Forces. All special unit members have the skills to work well with others. They need to stay physically fit, and they spend a great deal of time in areas that are far away from technology. And most of all, they need great mental and emotional strength to cope with challenges.

cannot let your emotions—depression or happiness, anxiety or excitement, anger or loneliness—get in the way of your performance. When you are focused on one goal and your mind is clear, things have a way of falling into place.

According to some military experts, a lack of mental preparation is the number-one reason why recruits fail training.

To pass Special Forces training, recruits have to be positive about life; they have to believe in themselves. This doesn't mean that the members of the Special Forces have no faults, but they are aware of their limitations and take action to do something about them.

Loose Ends

If you have any emotional issues with people close to you such as parents or significant others, you should try your best to resolve them before entering the military. Training is stressful enough without having to worry about a problem with a relationship.

MOTIVATION

Before you start a physical fitness program, you need mental **motivation**. Simply being unfit may supply the necessary motivation. Maybe you feel annoyed when you run out of breath easily or constantly feel tired. Compare yourself with other people of the same age and sex. Are they healthier and happier than you? Does their quality of life motivate you to become the best you can be?

Select a person you admire and ask yourself what it is about that person that you admire. Think about it. What qualities do you share with this person? Other people are

UNDERSTAND THE FULL MEANING

motivation: The reason or reasons a person acts the way he does.

DID YOU KNOW?
The soldier with a strong character will always bounce back from defeat. After a setback, your motivation should become even stronger.

mirrors in which you can see yourself. However, do not just copy other people. Work out what it is that you like about this individual and concentrate on developing these qualities in yourself. Also, look at what is weak about this person and ask yourself if you have these weaknesses too.

Once you begin your training program, you can start to experiment with different exercise routines to suit you. Think about your goals and then go for them. Set yourself sensible challenges and celebrate when you achieve them.

CRITICISM

Criticism can be painful but it can also help you to see yourself as other people see you. Keep in mind that if you were in the Special Forces, being grilled by a commanding officer would be par for the course. One of the most important skills to learn during training is not to take criticism personally. Your trainers are not insulting you as a person. Often they are trying to tear down all of your inner defenses to see if you will crack. Don't let them. Take what they say with a grain of salt.

Retired U.S. Army Lt. Col. Dave Grossman speaks to Airmen about the psychological and physiological preparation for combat Feb. 10, 2010, at Cannon Air Force Base, N.M. Grossman is briefing Airmen on the stress and mindset for combat situations. The briefing is for Airmen who are most likely to deploy to a combat environment and operate outside a base perimeter.

Up is Down / Black is White

When you first enter training, the way things are done may not always make complete sense to you. In fact, many things will seem upside down. Your instructor may ask you to perform a task that makes no sense to you. Try your best not to go into training with any preconceived ideas of what your lifestyle should be like. Expectations get in the way of reality and can interfere with your ability to adapt to your new circumstances.

You can also learn to give yourself **constructive** criticism. This doesn't mean that you put yourself down. Instead, it means that you learn to see yourself realistically, confident in your ability to grow and change.

Use the power of your imagination to shape your character. For example, think about how you would cope with a dangerous situation. Imagine that you are in the Special Forces, hiking across Afghanistan—and you end up getting lost in the hills and then breaking your leg. Now imagine that a storm breaks. Picture how you would cope under these circumstance. Be as realistic as you can be. The point is not to fantasize yourself into the role of a super hero, but rather to imagine how you would actually react if you were in that set of circumstance. Since you're not actually lost, cold, and in pain, you'll have the advantage over someone who is truly in a difficult situation, and this allows you to make full use of your mind's creative abilities to problem solve. This isn't just a game of make-believe. Mental activities like this can help you train yourself to be strong.

SENSE OF HUMOR

British Air Marshall Hugh Sidney called humor "necessary armor." Having a sense of humor is essential for elite soldiers, allowing them to cope with otherwise unbearable situations. All elite soldiers experience setbacks, upsets, disappoint-

UNDERSTAND THE FULL MEANING

constructive: Helpful; useful for improving or making something better.

US Marine Corps (USMC) Staff Sergeant (SSGT) Daniel L. Tompkins, a Drill Master grades recruits during their final drill.

ments, and catastrophes—but humor gives them a sense of distance from their problems and lightens their mood.

Use the benefits of laughter when you need it most. If you can develop the ability to laugh at yourself, you will not become so angry or frustrated that you lose control of your reactions.

DID YOU KNOW?
Scientific studies have found that those who laugh more are less depressed, feel less alone, and have lower levels of stress.

This is not to say that recruits don't need to take combat training seriously. They should. However, when your face is stuck in the mud, keeping a smile on your face can make the difference between success and failure.

A Healthy Sense of Distance

Don't depend on your circumstances to define your identity. Instead, always remain a little distant from what's going on around you. You are not your circumstances. Remind yourself that your identity will remain once your circumstances have changed, and all experiences are only temporary. A healthy sense of humor and the ability to let go of the small stuff (rather than becoming upset over small frustrations) are also effective strategies for achieving a healthy distance from your surroundings.

Keeping a positive attitude is the best insurer of success. If you can think positively, keep on moving forward, and laugh when disaster strikes, you can eventually attain your goals.

OVERCOMING FEAR

Feeling scared is a natural response to the challenges Special Force units face. Don't be ashamed if you too have times when you feel fear. Everyone get scared sometimes!

Here are a couple of tips to help you overcome fear:

- Put problems in perspective. Imagine how you will feel about this situation five or ten years from now, regardless of what happens. Few incidents or decisions have a lasting effect on our lives. Become **philosophical** about life. Think of life as a constant cycle of joy and sorrow, success and defeat, frustration and achievement.

- Use the power of **visualization**. Imagine confronting a situation that makes you feel anxious. Picture the scene in your mind; be as detailed as you can be; and then imagine yourself handling the situation and getting past it.

CHALLENGING SITUATIONS

Special Operations units deal with situations that most people could not handle. Imagine hiding in a jungle behind

UNDERSTAND THE FULL MEANING

philosophical: Reasonable and rational; calm and sensible.

visualization: Forming a mental image of something.

The Mental Effects of War

John Brosius suffers from post-traumatic stress disorder (PTSD). That's why he has the words "Not all wounds are visible" tattooed on his arm.

In 1994, he participated in Haiti for Operation Uphold Democracy, when the United States provided assistance to Haiti after a violent overthrow of the democratically elected government. John was a paratrooper with the Third Special Forces, which is a specialized group of soldiers that train foreign military units. While he was in Haiti, he saw women and children suffer, and he was in an armed confrontation he won't talk about. Ever since then, PTSD symptoms, which include anxiety, panic attacks, and depression, have haunted him.

PTSD has no cure. Therapy only lessens the symptoms. But soldiers are trained to keep their heads up and perform their duty. Even though John suffers from PTSD, he still has the spirit of a warrior. He knows that PTSD is just another sort of wound, a mark of his service to his country.

enemy lines for an **indefinite** period of time. How would you survive? How would you ensure you weren't caught? How would you eat or sleep? How would you hold on to the hope that you would be rescued? Perhaps you could imagine being a **pararescueman** and saving a downed soldier's life while shots are fired at you.

These are extreme situations, but they happen to members of the military in special units each day. You can learn the skills necessary to cope with extreme circumstances like these by developing the ability to handle ordinary real-life challenges—like failing a driving test, breaking up with a girlfriend or boyfriend, having a fight with your parents, or losing out on an after-school job you'd hoped to get. Learning to deal with these everyday stresses will allow you to develop the mental strength to face extreme situations.

How to Handle Panic

A psychiatrist in Japan created a three-step exercise that helps his patients cope with panic. It can be applied to the stress that comes with training for the Special Forces—and it works for everyday anxiety as well. The three steps are:

- Stand or sit upright.
- Take a deep breath through the mouth, filling your lungs.
- Exhale very slowly through the nose. Imagine that you are holding a feather in front of your nose and exhale so gently that the "feather" remains perfectly still."

That's it! It sounds simple, but it works.

UNDERSTAND THE FULL MEANING

indefinite: Uncertain, without a fixed limit.

pararescueman: A Special Forces operative who has been trained to carry out rescue operations and give emergency medical treatment, both in civilian and military situations.

CHAPTER 3

How Elite Units Are Chosen

For the first time in many years, the Army is recruiting civilians to join the U.S. Special Forces. This means you can enlist on a Special Forces contract, which puts you in the pipeline for the required Special Forces training program.

To qualify for the Special Forces contract you must meet the following criteria:

- Be a male between the ages of twenty and thirty. (Special Forces positions are not open to women.)

- Be a U.S. citizen.

- Have a high school diploma.

- Achieve a General Technical score of 110 or higher and a combat operation score of 98 on the Armed Services Vocational Aptitude Battery (ASVAB). Scoring high on the ASVAB is key to being able to join the

U.S. Special Forces. It also makes a difference when it comes to enlistment bonuses.

- Qualify for a secret-level security clearance.

- Qualify and volunteer for Airborne training.

- Take the Defense Language Aptitude Battery or Defense Language Proficiency Test.

- Achieve an overall minimum score of 229 on the Army Physical Fitness Test (APFT).

Recruits are carefully chosen for the elite forces. Only men with mental and physical stamina will be able to succeed.

DID YOU KNOW?

To join the military, one of the first challenges you will have is to show that you have some basic knowledge and skills by scoring well on the Armed Services Vocational Aptitude Battery (ASVAB). The ASVAB is made up of several verbal, math, and technical tests. The ASVAB was developed by the Department of Defense, and it is given at over 14,000 schools and Military Entrance Processing Stations nationwide. You will need a strong combined score to be considered for the Special Forces.

You can take practice ASVAB tests at www.military.com/ASVAB. These practice tests will give you an idea of how you'd score on the actual test and show you areas where you need to improve. The website also has study guides to help you prepare for the ASVAB test. Scoring high takes concentration and study.

The military wants people who will go on when others give up and who have the level of intelligence needed to operate sophisticated tools and weapons. Units like the Navy SEALs and the Green Berets have high standards of excellence. The military commits a lot of time, money, and energy to train-

Students assigned to a Basic Underwater Demolition/SEAL class participate in rock portage at Coronado Island. Rock portage is one of many physically demanding evolutions that are a part of First Phase training.

ing new units. That's why they are very selective about who they train: they don't want to waste their time and money on someone who won't be able to make it!

Military recruiters have an eye out for a specific set of qualities when they're looking for elite soldiers. This includes aggression, physical fitness, and team spirit. Since most modern elite units fight in small groups at the forefront of the battle or behind enemy lines, these soldiers need **self-discipline**, motivation, intelligence, and **initiative**. They must be dependable and **self-reliant** in combat.

SELF-RELIANCE

Obviously, these soldiers must also have specialized skills, and they must know **field tactics**, but senior officers know that the ability to act independently is the foundation for these skills. So much is at stake when special forces are performing operations: defense of country, as well as life itself. Members of the elite forces will often have no one to turn

UNDERSTAND THE FULL MEANING

self-discipline: The ability to train and control yourself, in order to help yourself become better.

initiative: The ability to take the first step to do something, as well as to follow through with it.

self-reliant: Independent; relying on yourself and your own skills, abilities, and resources.

field tactics: The maneuvers and actions used in combat and in any operations away from command headquarters.

to but themselves when a crisis arises; their commanding officer won't be there to give them instructions. They need to be able to make decisions on their own. That's why you won't hear many pep talks in the special forces. The military wants individuals who motivate themselves.

HANDLING OBSTACLES

Becoming a member of Special Forces is not an easy task. Commanding officers purposefully make it as hard as possible. This is because recruits are being tested at the same time they are being trained. If you can't handle the challenges of training, you definitely won't be able to handle the rigors of special ops.

COURAGE

Physical strength and endurance are important for your survival in the Special Forces, but senior officers are looking for qualities beyond your physical abilities. As a result, you might end up training in the wilderness, where you are forced to solve problems on your own for weeks at a time. This takes intelligence and physical stamina, but it also takes courage.

How would you define courage? It doesn't mean that you won't ever feel scared—because you will (and you should!). The military defines courage as the determination and commitment to keep going even when it gets tough. That's what it takes to go far in the Special Forces.

Green Beret troops, Staff Sgt. John J. Sanchez and Sgt. Rodney Allen, left to right, rappel down an icy mountain.

DID YOU KNOW?

Besides being part of the world's most highly trained military force, other SF benefits include an enlistment bonus of up to $20,000 and over $70,000 to further your education.

SPECIFIC REQUIREMENTS FOR BECOMING A GREEN BERET

The first step is to pass the Special Forces Assessment and Selection Course (SFAS). To get into this course, you must meet some basic physical fitness requirements by scoring a minimum of 206 on the Army physical fitness test for the 17-to-21 age group.

Remember, that's the minimum score. If you're serious about applying for Special Forces, never settle for the minimum score in anything. Since the Green Berets are so **selective** and **competitive**, you should try to stand out in as many areas as you can.

The U.S. military website (www.military.com) recommends that you work toward these goals before trying to join the

UNDERSTAND THE FULL MEANING

selective: Discriminating; making selections based on a narrow set of criteria.

competitive: Liking to compete; trying consistently to do better than others and than you have in the past.

DID YOU KNOW?

If you dream of being in a special unit, start by getting real-life experience in the military. Recruits who show an unusually high level of ability in basic training may catch the eye of senior officers. Even if you start out with a military job that doesn't particularly appeal to you, make up your mind to excel in it. If you do, you'll be taking the first steps toward the Special Forces.

Special Forces:

- Complete the 2-mile run in at least 12 to 14 minutes.
- Be able to do 100 sit-ups in 2 minutes.
- Be able to do 100 push-ups in 2 minutes.

Accomplishing these goals will bring you close to a perfect score of 300 and increase your chances of being selected for SFAS.

The three-week SFAS course, taught at Fort Bragg, North Carolina, consists of two phases. The first phase involves physical training. You will be expected to run; swim; do sit-ups, pull-ups, and push-ups; run an obstacle course; and participate in rucksack marches and **orienteering** exercises. The second phase measures your leadership and teamwork abilities. Twenty-five days of continuous mental and physical

UNDERSTAND THE FULL MEANING

orienteering: Finding your way using a map and a compass.

stress persuade the poorly motivated to leave at the beginning of the selection process. Only about half of an average class of 300 candidates pass SFAS.

REQUIREMENTS FOR BECOMING A NAVY SEAL

To apply to the Navy SEALs you must be able to perform a minimum of 42 push-ups in two minutes. After that, you must do 50 sit-ups in two minutes and be able to perform 6 pull-ups. A Navy SEAL must also be able to run 1.5 miles—wearing boots and long pants—in under 11 minutes and 30 seconds.

An obstacle course at the Naval Special Warfare Center (NSWC) in San Diego. The obstacle course is an integral part of training cycles for U.S. Navy SEALs at NSWC.

CHAPTER 4
Special Forces Training

The opportunity to change history through the Special Forces is not available to everyone. The military only selects a chosen few to go through training—and not everyone makes it through training.

Many are simply not able to take the pressure. For instance, in a part of military SEAL training known as "hell week," trainees are deprived of sleep and intentionally malnourished for a short time to make sure that each recruit is able to work as a team when everything else fell apart. The Navy SEALs also lose from 70 to 80 percent of their recruits during training. Ten percent of the students don't have the physical ability to make it through, and another group, about 10 to 15 percent, will only make it through training if they are not injured. Ranger school has a similar rate of graduation: only 25 percent of rangers are able to complete all phases of training.

So what is the difference between those who make it and those who don't? Motivation. If you come into training with the attitude of a warrior who can overcome any obstacle, you have won half the battle.

GREEN BERET TRAINING

Once a candidate has passed the Special Forces Assessment and Selection (SFAS) course, he is eligible for the Special Forces Qualification Course (also known as the "Q" Course). This course is divided into three phases: Small Unit Tactics, Military Occupational Skill (MOS) Specific Training, and a Culmination Exercise that includes a field exercise called "Robin Sage," where the candidates will be asked to demonstrate all the skills they have learned on the course.

The Small Unit Tactics phase lasts forty-six days. It concentrates on the basic crafts for a career behind enemy lines. The candidates are taught **navigation**, field craft, unarmed combat, small-unit tactics, and live-fire exercises. During this phase, the selectors watch the candidates carefully. They note the applicant's ability to absorb information, and they also look at their level of discipline and self-reliance.

Students are divided up into groups at the beginning of the next phase. Each trains in different skills: weapons, communications, engineering, or combat medicine. This will be

UNDERSTAND THE FULL MEANING

navigation: The ability to find your way in various landscapes and environments.

the soldier's essential role within his twelve-man "A-Team" unit. Officers have their own training detachment, which teaches advanced combat tactics. The officer course trains soldiers in the skills and knowledge required to be commanders. The weapons course drills soldiers in all types of foreign weapons, from rifles to antitank guns; students of the engineering course are taught field construction and fortification, land mine warfare, target analysis, and demolitions. Secret communications are also vital for the resupply,

Special forces soldiers operate as members of a team—each member has a role to play. This soldier is participating in a special course in combat medicine.

reinforcement. and escape of Special Forces teams behind enemy lines. To pass the signals course, the students must show they can build radio antennae, make and break secret codes, and use specialized communications equipment. At the end of the course, the students must be able to send and receive Morse code at a minimum speed of eight words per minute. In medicine training, soldiers get a "mini-medical degree," which covers subjects from anatomy to physiology to veterinary medicine and war surgery. Most courses last sixty-five days. Combat medicine is the longest course, lasting for twenty-one weeks.

Daily training during the "Q" Course takes it toll on the body, since the day usually starts very early and ends late. Most people who quit the course lack the ability to focus through the fatigue and stress that accompanies such training.

Training toughens up a student. It helps him be able to **persevere** through seemingly impossible situations. To learn this, trainees go through difficult conditions, including forced sleep deprivation. Dealing with **simulated** physical hardship creates a bond between students, one that will stay when they enter actual special operations in the field. Above all, special operations teach teamwork.

The culmination exercise is the last phase of the "Q" Course and is designed to test the skills learned in the other

UNDERSTAND THE FULL MEANING

persevere: To continue on in spite of hardships and difficulties.

simulated: Something that has been imitated or recreated to be like the real thing.

two phases. The Robin Sage Field Training Exercise lasts nineteen days and simulates a realistic wartime operation. Organized into "A-teams," the students must train a mock guerrilla force comprised of civilians from local families. Once trained and organized, the "guerillas" are led on a series of raids and ambushes against the 82nd Airborne Division, who play the forces of the "evil dictator."

Survivors of the "Q" Course are awarded their green berets. The "Special Forces" shoulder tabs are awarded only to those candidates who pass the final two phases: Language Training and Survival, Evasion, Resistance, and Escape (SERE).

DID YOU KNOW?

The SEALs can be sent anywhere the United States needs a special operation. Some units specialize in working in a specific continent or area in the world. Navy SEALs are prepared at any time that military intervention is needed. Within the past few years, the SEALs have assisted the Navy and Army in our two most recent wars: Afghanistan and Iraq.

They have also aided the United States in specialized missions, such as in April of 2009, when Somali pirates took over an American ship. The specialized forces proved just how efficient they were when they rescued the entire crew by using SEAL snipers positioned on a Navy boat 100 feet away. Lt. Nathan Potter, a spokesman for the Naval Special Warfare Command, later commented on the three simultaneous sniper shots: "I've been hearing that it was a lucky shot but this is what they're trained for."

NAVY SEALS

The Navy Seals are one of the hardest organizations to get into, since immense amounts of endurance and determination are needed to carry out Navy SEAL missions. Once an applicant has been chosen, the real training begins.

The first phase of SEAL training lasts eight weeks. During this phase, the commanding officer trains, develops, and **assesses** candidates. They must be comfortable in the water, work as a team, and make their bodies fit. The physical tasks, which include running, swimming, and calisthenics, become harder and harder as time goes on. Recruits

Cost of Training a SEAL

The Navy SEALs are selective about whom they train because training a single Navy SEAL can cost up to $500,000. Devoting a large amount of money and time to train a single person comes with risk; the military wants to be sure it makes the best investment.

take weekly 4-mile timed runs; they make their way across timed obstacle courses; and they swim long distances. The fourth week of phase one, called "hell week," is the hardest. This is when the military sees if a candidate for the SEALs will crack under pressure. To do this, the officers put their

UNDERSTAND THE FULL MEANING

assesses: Evaluates, judges, determines the value or character of something.

A third phase student in Basic Underwater Demolitions/SEAL (BUDS) training is illuminated by a flare during a night shoot on San Clemente Island. The third phase of BUDS focuses on land warfare and includes training in pistol, rifle, demolitions and tactical movement.

trainees a week that simulates what an actual high-stress mission would be like.

In the second phase of training, SEAL candidates condition themselves to be combat swimmers. Trainers focus on

Polo Players

In 2010, Navy recruiters funded a study to find what group of people would be most eligible to be a member of the SEALs. The results came in, and water polo players made the top of the list. The amount of time that water polo players spend in the water and the way the sport uses different parts of the body and quick reflexes makes water polo players ideal candidates to be Navy SEALs.

scuba diving skills. While the trainees learn techniques for diving, they continue extensive physical exercise.

The third phase lasts nine months. This phase trains candidates in the use of weapons and explosives. After the instruction on combat, trainers continue to make physical tasks harder and the running distances become longer. In the final three and a half weeks of training, the trainee applies all of the techniques that he has learned.

If you are interested in joining the Navy SEALs, there is a wealth of information on the Internet. One good source

UNDERSTAND THE FULL MEANING

demolition: Relating to the use of explosives.

stealth: Moving and acting secretly and without being detected.

amphibious: Military operations taking place both on land and in water.

is information.usnavyseals.com. The official website for the SEALs is www.sealswcc.com. Also, one can go to a nearby recruitment office for more specific questions on joining and preparing for the SEALs.

ARMY RANGERS

The Army Rangers are a specialized team of light infantry-men who carry out ambushes and other special maneuvers by land, sea, or air. Any eighteen-year-old male may apply to the Rangers when enlisting for the military. Specialized training can take from one and a half to two years.

In order to become an Army Ranger, you must score above 80 percent on the Army Physical Fitness Test, and 70 percent or higher on all other military exams. You also must complete the Combat Water Survival Assessment and must be able to complete a 15-meter swim with boots and other equipment, as well as a 12-mile road march in three hours or less.

After being accepted as an applicant, the recruit goes through Ranger School, a sixty-one-day combat leadership course. In Ranger School, soldiers learn skills that include navigation, **demolition**, and **stealth**. In the beginning phase, soldiers learn military skills, physical and mental endurance, stamina, and confidence. In the mountain phase, Ranger students learn the principles and techniques for employing small combat units in a mountain environ-ment. The students learn how to plan, prepare, and execute combat operations in mountainous regions. They also learn mountain survival techniques.

Army Rangers trainees crossing a rope bridge during the water navigation skill phase of combat control training. Combat control training teaches the fundamentals of water and land navigation, equipment operations and survival skills.

DID YOU KNOW?
If you're interested in joining the Special Forces, check out the official army website, www.goarmy.com/special_forces.

Rangers learn how to operate under physically and mentally demanding, high-stress situations. Training develops the student's ability to plan units and lead them in different scenarios. Many of those scenarios involve difficult-to-maneuver situations, including airborne, air assault, amphibious, and small boats.

More information on how to join the Rangers can be found on the Internet at www.military.com/army-rangers/join. The site gives guidelines for joining and contains other links for those interested in becoming Rangers.

PSYOP

PYSOP stands for Psychological Operations. PSYOP members deal with winning over the hearts of citizens in enemy countries and discouraging the military soldiers they are

DID YOU KNOW?
Psychological Operations Specialists acquire many skills that will aid them in life, even after their military career is over. They will learn how to conduct research, develop media products, gain computer skills, and prepare reports.

fighting. They work to influence opinions and attitudes for the military as well as aid combat soldiers using unconventional combat techniques. In wartime, for example, a PSYOP

When Psychology Backfires

PSYOP members today can expect to be sent any place where active military operations are going on. Psychological operations units have been used on the major fronts for America's twenty-first-century wars in Iraq and Afghanistan. Sometimes, however, psychological warfare has unexpected results. In April of 2010, for example, a PSYOP unit in Afghanistan began playing Metallica, The Offspring, and Thin Lizzy to annoy the Taliban. Whenever an insurgent would open fire, the United States army would blast country, heavy metal, and rock for up to a mile in the city of Marjah. While few doubt that the music irritated the Taliban, it also bothered many Afghani children and did little to win public support for the occupation. As a result, PSYOP decided to discontinue the strategy.

member may design a leaflet to drop into enemy territory. PSYOP performs a wide variety of tasks; some are very close to combat—for instance, creating a barrage of confusing sounds to be played loudly on the battlefield—and some are more removed from actual fighting—such as creating a

DID YOU KNOW?

Anyone interested in joining Psychological Operations special forces can go to go to the website www.goarmy.com/JobDetail.do?id=7 for more information on recruitment.

pro-American website accessible to citizens of an unfriendly country.

PSYOP members must have an aptitude for college-level study in the social sciences. They must be interested in foreign cultures and languages, and proficient in researching information from the Web and printed materials. Candi-

PSYOP in Peace Time

Psychological Operations can also be applied in situations without any combat involved. These units provide information to others in times of disaster or crisis. For instance, PSYOP forces delivered necessary information within the U.S. after Hurricane Andrew in 1992. Tactical Psychological Operations teams (TPTs) sent out information by loudspeaker on the location of relief shelters and other necessities.

dates should also be able to write and speak clearly. Creative talent is useful as well.

Joining Psychological Operations requires nine weeks of Basic Combat Training. There, the trainee will learn the basic skills of a soldier. Next, he will go through fourteen weeks of Advanced Individual Training (AIT), where he learns skills to be a Psychological Operations Specialist. After graduation from AIT come three weeks of airborne training and four to six months of language training. Reserve PSYOP Specialists, however, are not required to go through airborne or language training for qualification.

THAT OTHERS MAY LIVE: PARARESCUE

The special operations unit of the U.S. Air Force that's in charge of rescue missions using parachutes is called Para-rescue. Pararescue is a difficult branch of the Air Force to

Pararescuemen AKA PJs

Special Forces servicemen in the United States are called officially called Pararescuemen, but ever since the 1940s, when they air-dropped to save a downed aircrew on the China-Burma border, they have been nicknamed the PJs. short for Para-Jumpers.

join. Their official website states that to join the Pararescue-men you must be able to:

- Swim 25 meters underwater on one breath.
- Swim 1,000 meters using the sidestroke or freestyle in 26 minutes or less.
- Run 1.5 miles in under 10 minutes and 30 seconds.
- Do eight chin-ups a minute or less.
- Do 50 sit-ups in two minutes or less.
- Complete 50 flutter kicks in two minutes or less.

DID YOU KNOW?

The website www.specialtactics.com/pararescue.shtml is an excellent resource for joining a pararescue unit.

The website also suggests that there are other ways to stand out from other applicants:

- Run three miles in under 21 minutes.
- Do 50 to 60 correct push-ups in two minutes.
- Do 100 to 130 sit-ups in a four-minute period.
- Do 12 pull-ups or chin-ups correctly.
- Swim 1500 meters in less than 28 minutes.

If a candidate is accepted, he must then go through a training period that lasts for almost a year. All recruits receive training to become fully qualified emergency medical technicians. They also learn advanced land navigation, light weapons usage, escape techniques, and survival techniques. Pararescuemen learn chemical warfare survival and various medical rescue techniques appropriate for warfare situations.

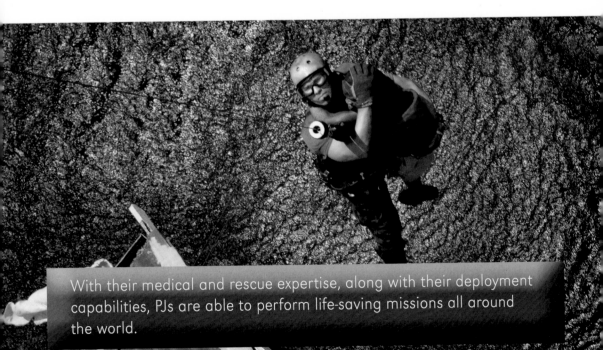

With their medical and rescue expertise, along with their deployment capabilities, PJs are able to perform life-saving missions all around the world.

Profile: Why Join Pararescue Forces?

When Ben Priddy, a twenty-one-year-old from Elizabeth-town, Kentucky, was interviewed by a local newspaper, the *News Enterprise*, he talked about why he chose to join a Special Forces unit. One reason was simple: joining the pararescumen was the best paying and most respected job available. Eighty-five percent of applicants are not able to complete pararescue training, but Ben looked forward to the challenge and the "adrenaline kick." Ben also stated that he was attracted to the fact that the military program focused on saving life instead of ending it.

Pararescuemen do not always operate in combat situations. For instance, in January of 2010, the United States Special Forces helped the Haitian government rescue victims of an earthquake. With the help of international teams, they rescued a total of 134 people.

MAKING HISTORY

The opportunity to make history—that's what you'll find in the elite forces. Passing the selection process is not easy, and training can be just as difficult. It takes a rare type of person to complete the training for elite units. Most people do not get to become a member of an elite unit even after they have been selected for training. But elite soldiers are not superhumans who were born able to perform on the battlefield like Rambo. They are people who dedicated themselves to excellence.

FIND OUT MORE ON THE INTERNET

Air Force www.airforce.com

Army Recruiting www.goarmy.com

Department of Defense www.defense.gov

Marine Corps www.marines.com

Navy www.navy.com

West Point www.usma.edu

The websites listed on this page were active at the time of publication. The publisher is not responsible for websites that have changed their address or discontinued operation since the date of publication. The publisher will review and update the websites upon each reprint.

FURTHER READING

Bryant, Russ. *To Be a U.S. Army Ranger.* Minneapolis, Minn.: Zenith Press, 2003.

Couch, Dick. *Chosen Soldier: The Making of a Special Forces Warrior.* New York: Three Rivers Press, 2008.

Couch, Dick. *The Finishing School: Earning the Navy SEAL Trident.* New York: Three Rivers Press, 2005.

De Lisle, Mark. *Special Ops Fitness Training: High-Intensity Workouts of Navy Seals, Delta Force, Marine Force Recon and Army Rangers.* Berkeley, Calif.: Ulysses Press, 2008.

Hollenbeck, Cliff. *To Be a U.S. Navy SEAL.* Minneapolis, Minn.: Zenith Press, 2003.

Martin, Joseph J. *Get Selected for Special Forces: How to Successfully Complete Assessment & Selection*. Arlington, Va.: Warrior Mentor, 2005.

Schumacher, Gerry. *To Be a U.S. Army Green Beret.* Minneapolis, Minn.: Zenith Press, 2005.

Stillwell, Alexander. *Elite Forces Manual of Mental and Physical Endurance: How to Reach Your Physical and Mental Peak.* New York: St. Martin's, 2006.

U.S. Navy. *U.S. Navy SEAL Guide to Fitness and Nutrition.* New York: Skyhorse, 2007.

BIBILIOGRAPHY

AllSands.com. "Mental Preparation For Military Basic Training," www.allsands.com/college/basictraining_ku_gn.htm (5 May 2010).

Fisher-Thompson, Jim. "U.S. Military Helped Search-and-Rescue Efforts in Haiti," www.america.gov/st/develop-english/2010/January/201001280958281ejrehsiF0.3818476.html (29 April 2010).

The News-Enterprise. "Priddy going into pararescue training," www.thenewsenterprise.com/cgi-bin/c2.cgi?053+article+News.Local+20100323163046053053002 (22 April 2010).

N.Y. Daily News. "Three Navy SEALS freed Capt. Phillips from pirates with simultaneous shots from 100 feet away," www.nydailynews.com/news/national/2009/04/14/2009-04-14_seals_freed_phillips_with_simultaneous_shots.html (22 April 2010).

60 Minutes. "Green Berets Recount Deadly Taliban Ambush," www.cbsnews.com/stories/2008/04/18/60minutes/main4026734.shtml?tag=contentMain;contentBody (28 April 2010).

U.S. Army. "Special Forces," www.goarmy.com/special_forces/qualifications_and_benefits.jsp (21 April 2010).

U.S. Army. "Special Operations Command," www.soc.mil (21 April 2010).

USAF Pararescue. "Is PARARESCUE Training For You?," www.pararescue.com/recruiting.aspx (21 April 2010).

Volkin, Michael. "Coping With Your First Day of Basic Training," www.gruntsmilitary.com/cgi-bin/newsscript.pl?record=11 (5 May 2010).

INDEX

ABOUT THE AUTHOR

Jack Montana lives in upstate New York with his wife and three dogs. He writes on military survival, health, and wellness. He graduated from Binghamton University.

ABOUT THE CONSULTANT

Colonel John Carney, Jr. is USAF-Retired, President and the CEO of the Special Operations Warrior Foundation.

PICTURE CREDITS

Joint Multinational Training Command
  Christian Marquardt: pg. 47

United States Air Force: pg. 59
  Senior Airman Erik Cardenas: pg 27
  Senior Airman Sheila deVera: pg 8
  Staff Sgt. Bennie Davis III: pg. 34
  Staff Sgt. Lakisha A. Croley: pg.11

United States Army
  C. A. Thompson: pg. 54
  Tech. Sgt. Bob Wickley: pg. 40

United States Marine Corps
  Cpl. Dustin T. Schalue: pg. 17
  Cpl. Michael L. Haas: pg. 22

United States Navy
  Mass Communication Specialist 1st Class Joseph W. Pfaff: pg. 51
  Mass Communication Specialist 2nd Class Daniel Barker: pg. 43
  Mass Communication Specialist 2nd Class Kyle D. Gahlau: pp. 37, 44
  Mass Communication Specialist 3rd Class Blake Midnight
  Matt Mogle: pg. 15

To the best knowledge of the publisher, all images not specifically credited are in the public domain. If any image has been inadvertently uncredited, please notify Harding House Publishing Service, 220 Front Street, Vestal, New York 13850, so that credit can be given in future printings.